Once upon a time ...

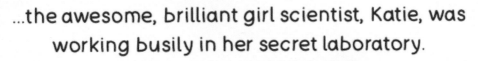

...the awesome, brilliant girl scientist, Katie, was
working busily in her secret laboratory.

Little did she know...

Somebody found out about her totally secret
laboratory and sneakily spied on her.

Katie's lab was filled with magical, colourful bottles. She loved mixing liquids. You name it and she has tried it. Every single invention had different, unknown effects.
At her experiment desk. She carefully poured chemicals which made wonderful sounds

WEE! BOOM! POW! Wow!

Each explosion made smoky, lavender clouds. After completing an invention, she would hold it up and say

"You are my greatest invention!"

in a dramatic voice – of course.

08:41am – a Saturday in April
This is when it all began.
While Katie was peacefully mixing inventions, she heard her mum's sing song voice.

Could Katie resist?

ABSOLUTELY NOT!

She dashed towards the stairs and she went to eat her breakfast, leaving her science lab unprotected.

"Come down for breakfast. I made your favourite: fried eggs and sausages".

Little did she know

Fifi the cat would take this opportunity to go slinking between her precious and dangerous inventions.

For the ordinary cat, this would have been PURRFECTLY fine but Fifi was no ordinary cat!

Fifi was a pedigree, Scottish fold. Katie's mum had bought her for £2000 and treated Fifi like a human! Fifi was Katie's furry older sister.
Fifi had home-cooked food, a human sized bed and only drank expensive water from glass bottles.
"Only the best for mama's fur baby" Mum would sing with pride

It would be fair to say that, Katie's mum was a

PURRFECT

cat lady and

TOO OVERPROTECTIVE!

As Katie ate her breakfast, Fifi was up to mischief.

She was as mischievous as a squirrel and as sneaky as a fox.

She jumped on the shelves. Inventions wobbled and fell. Fifi then, sniffed, rubbed, tapped

AND EVENTUALLY...

Drank one!

When she did, her fur shot out like rockets. Her eyes glowed like lightbulbs in the dark. Then she started to grow. She grew as big as a double decker bus. Katie's precious, mysterious inventions crashed to the floor of the lab! If only Katie knew, she wouldn't have enjoyed her breakfast.

Katie was excitedly munching on her breakfast then the house shook angrily. Katie and her mum thought it was their neighbour as he loved D.I.Y. Her mum shouted.

"You horrible neighbour! Stop trying to destroy my house, you monster!"

Little did she know...
The real culprit was her favourite daughter.

Katie's mum looked up at the clock and asked,...

"Katie, darling, have you seen Fifi anywhere? It's time for her breakfast."

Katie shook her head and grunted something. She didn't know.

"That's strange, she never misses her gnocchi and prawn breakfast," replied mum. Right then, Katie saw something purrculiar outside the kitchen window.

Feeling confused, she got up and opened the curtain. Katie saw a humongous, mischievous,

U.F.O (Unidentifiable, Furry Object).

In shock and terror. Katie ran up to the lab. She was greeted by the
sounds of glass breaking and slow dripping sounds
Potion bottles clanging on the floor: Crash! Boom! Pow!
It was a colossal cat-astrophe.
Little did she know,
things were going to get worse.

As her eyes adjusted to the dark, Katie cold see a **hu-hu-humongous** Fifi. She blinked over and over, hoping to unsee the terrible situation.

"Nope, not today!"
Unable to unsee the destruction – she decided it was best
to ignore the problem and went back to eat her breakfast.

Mum left and before Katie could think
about getting some rest, she heard
glass shattering loudly.
In a flash, Katie ran to the window to
see what was happening.
And what did she see?

Fifi was riding on a bus and heading towards town. Katie's jaw dropped to the floor. With the lab destroyed and the fur baby exploring town, it would be impossible to undo this mess without mum finding out.

Katie huffed and puffed, thinking about what to do. "If I don't turn Fifi back, mum will be upset. If Fifi does not come back, there will be consequences." At this point she could call her mum for help, call friends or chase after Fifi alone.

"Urgh!"

"I can do this!"
Deciding to do it on her own, she grabbed her
jacket from her bed.
Under her bed she pulled out an old water bottle.
It was labelled super-secret- in-case-of-
emergency-potion. (Of all the silly places)
She quickly ran to the door and made her way to
the town.

In town, Katie had to slide, shimmy and push through crowds of mums and buggies. Ducking into buildings and under bridges, she searched and searched.

"Girl you gotta Stay **PAWsitive**, the trouble
maker must be here. Think brain, think!"
Then she remembered a tip her teacher gave.
"If you are stuck and you can't see the answer –
use your ears."
In the distance, there was the sound of glass and
metal being crushed.

TINKLE CRASH CRUNCH

Following the sounds, she eventually found Fifi
scratching and pushing the buses at the bus station.
Thanks Mr. Henry
At last Katie found her naughty sister.
She shouted - "What do you think you're doing?
Come here this instant!"
For a moment - a brief moment. Fifi looked obedient
and Katie thought she was going to be a good girl.
Katie pulled out the super-secret- in-case-of-
emergency-potion.

The next thing Katie saw was a blur and felt a strong gust of wind. With great speed, Fifi jumped from the road to the buildings and disappeared.

By now people were coming out of the theatre and saw a few million pounds of broken buses and Katie. The confused crowds, stared at Katie as they walked past. Katie wished she was invisible at this point. She left a note and ran to chase Fifi.

JUU JUU JUUU

After the bus disaster, Katie searched in every shop and in every tunnel. She tried listening again but just heard the general city noises Speeding cars, Helicopters and Ambulances.

VROOM

To be honest, she gave up trying. Until... Something told her to look up. There at the top of the sky scraper

was... somebody furr-milliar

Fifi was trying to swat a helicopter. ARGH!!! Fifi was in play mode: claws out and 100% energy. If she continued like this, the town would be destroyed! The only thing that can stop Fifi from playing was

FOOD. Katie had a PAW-some plan.

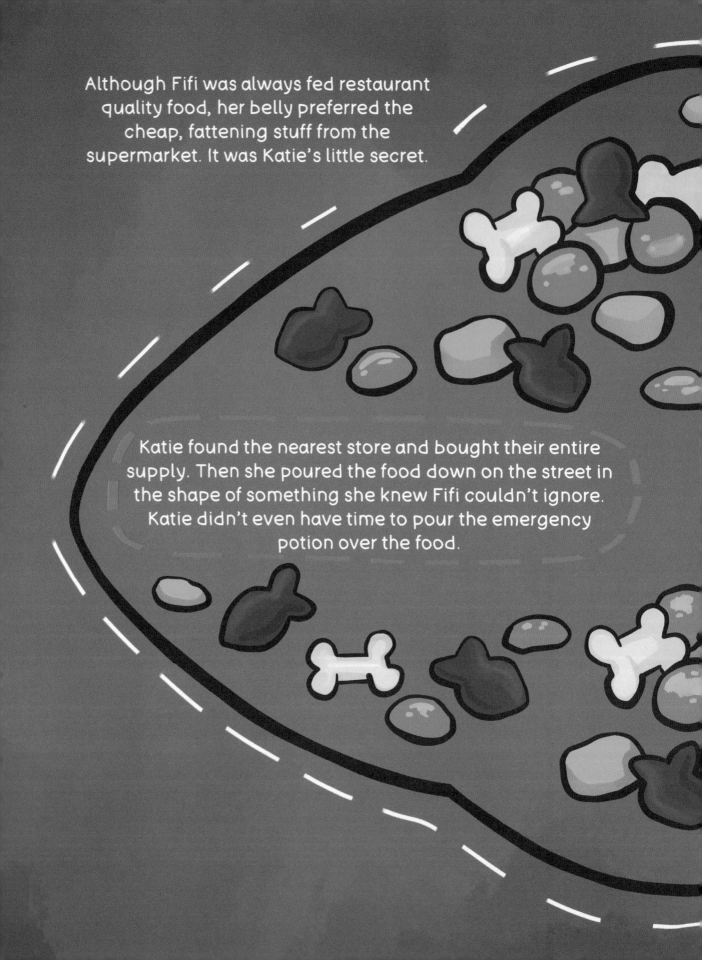

Although Fifi was always fed restaurant quality food, her belly preferred the cheap, fattening stuff from the supermarket. It was Katie's little secret.

Katie found the nearest store and bought their entire supply. Then she poured the food down on the street in the shape of something she knew Fifi couldn't ignore. Katie didn't even have time to pour the emergency potion over the food.

Fifi spotted her and immediately ran down. Like a vacuum she sucked up all the cat food.

And RAN!

"How could that cat!"

Katie become deflated to see Fifi run off for the
fourth time today.
She checked her phone for messages.
It was 2 O'clock and there was a message from
her BFF.

Katie could no longer try and catch Fifi alone. It
was time to call for help.
She quickly messaged back
"hEy KeLeSy Do YoU wAnNa PlAy HiDe AnD
sEeK wItH mE?" Katie said in funny language.
"Absolutely!" said Kelesy feeling joyful.

Both Katie and Kelsey met up at Kiddie Kingdom.
Katie explained everything that had happened.
"I wish I had called you sooner. I've wasted hours.
Only 1 hour left until, mum comes home."
Katie was excited to have Kelesy.
Kelesy was the undefeated Queen of hide-and-
seek, in their school.
She could find anything. Her specialties included
lost jumpers and cardigans, lost parents and lost
letters.

"Do you have any clues?" asked Kelesy.
"Fifi just ate so she was most likely sleeping near home in a cosy spot." Katie continued to sob.
"Katie, why don't you check Quality Street and I go check Cola Road?" suggested Kelesy.
Katie walked down Cola Road.
Kelesy took a stroll down Da Quality Street. She saw some quality spots and boxes but no Fifi. Although there were two of them looking, they both returned empty handed.

Katie asked "Hey Kels, aren't you the best at finding things?".
Kelesy said nothing. She was listening intensely.
Kelesy shushed Katie and crept towards the neighbour's house.
As she arrived on the neighbour's drive way, she said,
"Your Fifi is a formidable opponent but I've got her!"
Kelesy pointed to a very large skip. The covering of the skip
flapped about. Something or someone was snoring inside the
big yellow skip in front of her neighbour's house.

When they both looked inside, they
found Fifi sleeping peacefully.
A job well done.
The emergency potion worked and they
pulled the sleepy kitty out of the skip.

Happy ending, right?
Wrong!

As it happens, Mum was already home and had searched high and low for both daughters. Unable to find her daughters, she kept looking out of the front window to see them return.
All she saw was Katie pull Fifi from the skip and knew they'd been up to no good.
There was no time for celebrating. It was Mum's turn to huff and puff. Though she was happy to have her daughters back, there were consequences.

Grounded for a month with no electronic devices.
The only adventures Fifi and Katie would be having
were the indoor kind. Katie in her room and Fifi in hers.
Considering all the damaged they caused in Croydon,
things worked out really well.
Being grounded is just the thing Katie needed to focus
on her newest and greatest inventions.

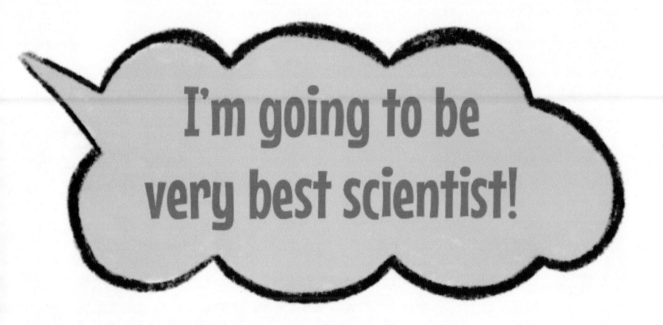

I wrote this story with my tutor.
I have read many books but only when I started
writing my story did, I learn an important lesson.

Not every story has its own happy ending.
The ending depends on the emotions you are
feeling when writing.

FRANCESKA S.